Polly and Ash
were in the woods
with Scrap.

Scrap got a stick.

It was the best stick of all.

But the stick was too long!

espresso
education

Phonics

Scrap's Best Stick

Sue Graves

W
FRANKLIN WATTS
LONDON·SYDNEY

First published in 2011 by
Franklin Watts
338 Euston Road
London NW1 3BH

Franklin Watts Australia
Level 17/207 Kent Street
Sydney NSW 2000

Text and illustration © Franklin Watts 2011

The Espresso characters are originated and
designed by Claire Underwood and Pesky Ltd.

The Espresso characters are the property of
Espresso Education Ltd.

A CIP catalogue record for this book is
available from the British Library.

ISBN: 978 1 4451 0431 7 (hbk)
ISBN: 978 1 4451 0444 7 (pbk)

Illustrations by Artful Doodlers Ltd.
Art Director: Jonathan Hair
Series Editor: Jackie Hamley
Series Designer: Matthew Lilly

Printed in China

Franklin Watts is a division of
Hachette Children's Books,
an Hachette UK company.

www.hachette.co.uk

Level 1 50 words
Concentrating on CVC words plus and, the, to

Level 2 70 words
Concentrating on double letter sounds and new letter
sounds (ck, ff, ll, ss, j, v, w, x, y, z, zz) plus no, go, I

Level 3 100 words
Concentrating on new graphemes (qu, ch, sh, th, ng,
ai, ee, igh, oa, oo, ar, or, ur, ow, oi, ear, air, ure, er)
plus he, she, we, me, be, was, my, you, they, her, all

Level 4 150 words
Concentrating on adjacent consonants (CVCC/CCVC
words) plus said, so, have, like, some, come, were, there,
little, one, do, when, out, what

The stick hit Polly's legs.

The stick hit Ash's legs.

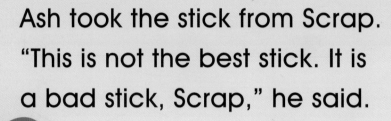

Ash took the stick from Scrap.
"This is not the best stick. It is
a bad stick, Scrap," he said.

Scrap was sad.

Just then, Polly saw
a nest in the grass.
A little chick was in
the nest.

"Look! The nest fell out of the tree," said Ash. "We must put the chick and the nest back up there," said Polly.

But the tree was
too high for
them to reach.

"What can we do?" said Polly.
"Let's put the nest on Scrap's
stick," said Ash. "We can push
the stick up into the tree."

19

Soon the nest
and the little chick
were back in the tree.
"Scrap, we like this
stick. It is the best stick
of all!" said Polly.

Puzzle Time

Match the words that rhyme to the pictures!

best

brick

nest

gong

stick

flee

crest

long

thick

song

test

tree

spree

Answers

nest – best, crest, test

long – gong, song

stick – brick, thick

tree – flee, spree

Espresso Connections

This book may be used in conjunction with the Literacy area on Espresso to secure children's phonics learning. Here are some suggestions.

Word Machine
Encourage children to play the Word Machine Level 2. Demonstrate how the machine works, and then move on to the activities.

Ask children to find the correct beginnings. Then ask children to find the correct endings.

Check that children are able to hear the difference between the letter sounds as different words come up.

Praise plausible attempts, such as substituting the letter "k" for "c" when attempting to find the hard c sound.

Spot the Word
Choose a book from the Big Book selection to play Spot the Word.

Give children pieces of paper with the high frequency words **said, so, have, like, some, come, were, there, little, one, do, when, out** or **what**. (The class could be split, with groups of children looking for different words.)

Ask children to note down on the paper each time they have seen or heard the word they are looking for.

At the end of the book, children should count up how many times their target word has been used.

Go back through the book together and see whether they got it right.

Praise plausible attempts, for example "live" for "like" and take the opportunity to point out why these words are different.

You could replicate the activity with this phonics story.